For Nicole and Jason—
love will keep you safe from the storm

First published in the United States of America in January 2015
by Bloomsbury Children's Books
www.bloomsbury.com

Bloomsbury is a registered trademark of Bloomsbury Publishing Plc

For information about permission to reproduce selections from this book, write to
Permissions, Bloomsbury Children's Books, 1385 Broadway, New York, New York 10018
Bloomsbury books may be purchased for business or promotional use. For information on bulk purchases please
contact Macmillan Corporate and Premium Sales Department at specialmarkets@macmillan.com

Library of Congress Cataloging-in-Publication Data
Yoon, Salina, author, illustrator.
Stormy night / by Salina Yoon.
pages   cm
Summary: Bear is frightened by a storm, but singing to his toy Floppy and being with his parents helps comfort him
until the storm goes to sleep, and so does he.
ISBN 978-0-8027-3780-9 (hardcover)
ISBN 978-0-8027-3807-3 (e-book) • ISBN 978-0-8027-3806-6 (e-PDF)
[1. Storms—Fiction. 2. Fear—Fiction. 3. Family life—Fiction. 4. Bedtime—Fiction. 5. Bears—Fiction.]
I. Title.
PZ7.Y817Sto 2015   [E]—dc23   2014012196

Art created digitally using Adobe Photoshop
Typeset in Triplex Sans
Book design by Nicole Gastonguay

Printed in China by Leo Paper Products, Heshan, Guangdong
1 3 5 7 9 10 8 6 4 2

STORMY NIGHT

Salina Yoon

BLOOMSBURY

NEW YORK   LONDON   NEW DELHI   SYDNEY

One stormy night,
Bear couldn't sleep.

The wind was whirring, the trees were crackling, and the rain was pounding against the windows.

"Don't worry," said Bear.
"I'll hold you tight. I'll keep you warm.
My love will keep you safe from the storm,"

he sang to his bunny, Floppy.

Bear felt better.

But when a thundering sound rumbled
through the forest, it startled Bear.

He sang his song again.

Mama came in to check on Bear. "May I stay with you tonight? I am so frightened by the storm!"

Bear was glad to see Mama.

He kissed Mama's nose to comfort her. Mama smiled.

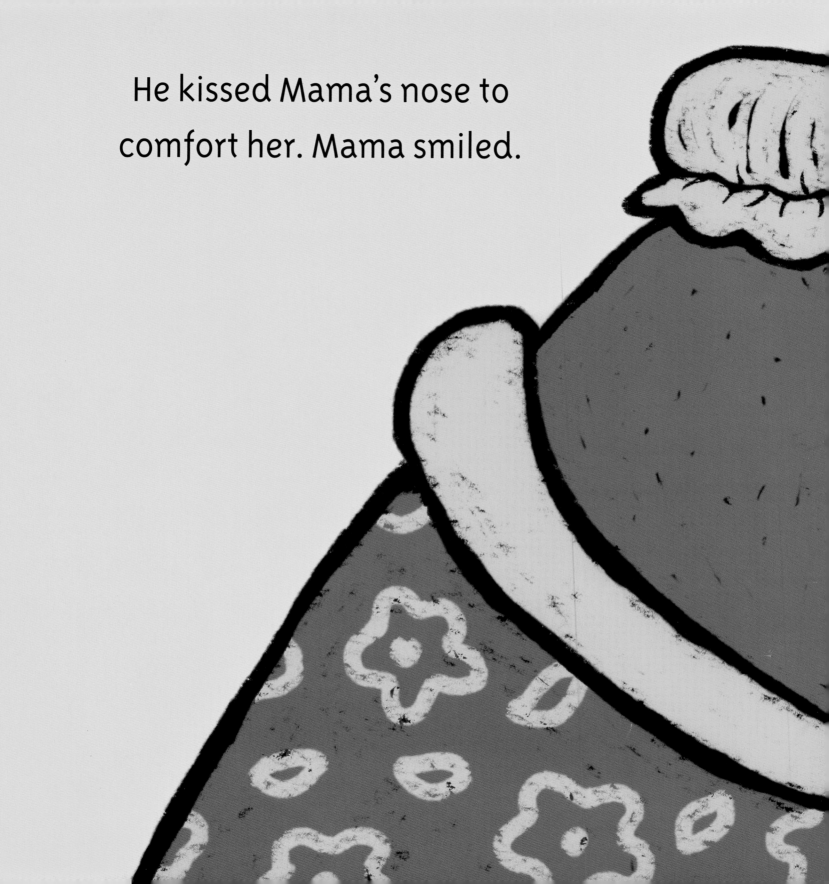

Bear felt better.

Then Papa came in to check
on Bear. "Is there room for me?
The storm is so loud tonight!"

Bear was glad to see Papa.
He tickled Papa's ear to comfort him.

Papa laughed! And Bear felt better.

"But what will make Floppy feel better?" thought Bear. "I know!"

"A book!"

Bear almost forgot about the storm until . . .

OM!

A loud, crashing sound of
thunder roared through the forest.

Bear shut his eyes tight.

Mama kissed his nose,

and Papa tickled his ear.

Mama sang to Bear just like
she did when he was a little cub.

"We'll hold you tight. We'll keep you warm.
Our love will keep you safe from the storm."
Bear felt better.

Bear yawned a sleepy yawn, and then it
was quiet. "What happened to the storm?"

"Even storms need their sleep!" said Papa.

And so do bears!